Skyler C. Gull

WRITTEN AND
ILLUSTRATED BY

ERIC ARMSTRONG

A Gully Gee Book

For Michael, Peggy, Bill, Elaine and Adrienne,
with special thanks to Carol Randolph of Studio R

Note for Librarians: a cataloguing record for this book that includes Dewey Decimal Classification and US Library of Congress numbers is available from the Library and Archives of Canada. The complete cataloguing record can be obtained from their online database at:
www.collectionscanada.ca/amicus/index-e.html
ISBN 978-1-4120-4968-9

Printed in Victoria, BC, Canada

 Trafford
PUBLISHING

Order online at: trafford.com/04-2776

10 9 8 7 6 5

One day,
Skyler C. Gull
watched kids
build sandcastles.
It looked like fun in the sun.

"I can make my own castle!"
Skyler blurted. "It will be cool."

The next morning, Skyler bought a shovel and pail at the store. He paid the cashier a sand dollar.

Back at the beach, Skyler shaped the sand for his creation. He got a sunburn on his bird beak. Ouch!

Skyler thought his new castle was awesome. It had everything he wanted — a tall, pointy roof and a balcony with a bird's-eye view. He couldn't wait to show his gull friend.

After Skyler woke up, he flew back to the beach. But his castle was gone. He just knew some dirty bird took it. "Whoa," Skyler squawked. "Some dude has stolen my sandcastle." His feathers were ruffled.

The next day, Skyler told the police about the crime. "This is, like, totally bogus," Skyler grumbled.

He offered a reward of 100 clams to whoever caught the crook. He wanted the sandcastle thief to be a jailbird.

His story made a big splash on the front page.

Daily Surf

Sandcastle Stolen!

By Starr Fish

That afternoon, Skyler built another castle.

This time, he tried to stay awake to keep watch, but the Sandman got in his eyes. He snoozed in the sun.

When Skyler was done sleeping, he couldn't believe his beady little eyes. His castle was gone! It looked like the sandcastle thief had struck again.

"Bummer," Skyler groused. "This is for the birds." He thought the robber was egging him on.

Skyler built another castle the next day. This time, he stayed awake to make sure nothing fishy happened.

He waited in the wings, but there was no sign of the culprit.

After a while, the high tide rolled in. "Surf's up, dude," Skyler screeched.

Closer and closer, the waves glided ashore. They splished and splashed and then …*whoosh!* The ocean washed Skyler's castle away. It was a wipe out.

Afterwards, Skyler felt like a loony bird. There wasn't a sandcastle thief after all. The tide was to blame.

Skyler knew he had to build his castle away from the high tide. But where? Suddenly, an idea hatched in his birdbrain.

Skyler thought his plan was egg-cellent.
"I'm so-oooo smart," Skyler bragged as he filled
up his pail with sand. He shook his tail feathers
and did the Seagull
Shuffle.
"Who's the
bird?" Skyler
chanted. "I'm the
bird. I'm the bird.
Uh-huh. Uh-huh."

Now, Skyler has
a brand new castle...